A Note from Miche

MY HO-HO-HO

CHRISTMAS

Hi! I'm Michelle Tanner. I'm nine years old. And my Christmas vacation is going to be ho-ho-horrible! That's because my cousin Marshall is coming to visit. And my dad says I have to keep Marshall busy.

Marshall is a total pain. He spills everything, he says *neato* all the time, and he loves bugs.

But I have a plan to save my Christmas. All I have to do is find someone else for Marshall to do stuff with. And that should be easy—because I have a very big family!

There's my dad and my two older sisters, D.J. and Stephanie. But that's not all.

My mom died when I was little. So my uncle Jesse moved in to help Dad take care of us. So did Joey Gladstone. He's my dad's best friend from college. It's almost like having three dads. But that's still not all!

First Uncle Jesse got married to Becky Donaldson. Then they had twin boys, Nicky and Alex. The twins are four years old now. And they're so cute.

That's nine people. Our dog, Comet, makes ten. Sure it gets kind of crazy sometimes. But I wouldn't change it for anything. It's so much fun to live in a full house!

FULL HOUSE™ MICHELLE novels

Available from MINSTREL Books

FULL HOUSE™
Michelle

My Ho-Ho-Horrible Christmas

Pauline Preiss

A Parachute Press Book

WB FAMILY ENTERTAINMENT™
R E A D I N G

A MINSTREL® BOOK

Published by POCKET BOOKS
New York   London   Toronto   Sydney   Tokyo   Singapore

A MINSTREL PAPERBACK *Original*

 A Minstrel Book published by
POCKET BOOKS, a division of Simon & Schuster Inc.
1230 Avenue of the Americas, New York, NY 10020

A PARACHUTE PRESS BOOK

 READING   Copyright © and ™ 1997 by Warner Bros.

ISBN: 0-671-00836-6

First Minstrel Books printing November 1997

10 9 8 7 6 5 4 3 2 1

Cover photo by Schultz Photography

Printed in the U.S.A.

My Ho-Ho-Horrible Christmas

Chapter 1

♥ "Please tell us what the big Christmas surprise is, Dad. Please, please, please!" Michelle begged. She straightened her bright red Santa hat over her strawberry blond hair.

"You'll find out soon enough," Danny answered.

"Come on, Dad," Michelle's thirteen-year-old sister, Stephanie, said. "You promised we'd get the big surprise today."

"Yeah, Dad," D.J. added. "You promised!" D.J. was Michelle's other big sister. She was eighteen—twice as old as Michelle—and went to college.

"The day's not over yet," Danny told them. "By the time we finish decorating the tree, the surprise should be here."

Michelle studied the Christmas tree. The colored lights blinked and twinkled. All the ornaments hung in place. Michelle smiled at the special ballerina ornament her dad gave her a few years ago. She loved that one. It was her very favorite.

We did a great job! Michelle thought. Everyone in the house helped decorate the tree—and that was a lot of people. Besides her dad and D.J. and Stephanie, there was Joey, and Michelle's uncle Jesse and aunt Becky, and their twins, Nicky and Alex.

Michelle's uncle Jesse moved in after Michelle's mother died. Michelle was just a little girl. She could hardly remember when Uncle Jesse *didn't* live with them.

Later Uncle Jesse got married, and Aunt Becky moved in. Michelle thought their little boys, Nicky and Alex, were super cute! She loved having Uncle Jesse and his family living on the third floor.

Joey Gladstone, her dad's best friend from college, moved in after Michelle's mom died too. He had an apartment in the basement. Michelle didn't want to think about what their house would be like without Joey. He was so much fun. He could always make her laugh.

We all worked really hard on the tree, Michelle thought. *But it still needs something. What's missing?* she wondered.

Tinsel! That's it! Michelle ripped open a big box of tinsel and threw a handful at the tree.

Michelle's dad rushed over and began separating the clump of tinsel. "Michelle! No throwing!" Danny exclaimed. "You have to put the tinsel on one strand at a time."

Jesse threw a wad of tinsel at Danny's head.

"Nice shot!" Stephanie called.

"No, no, no!" Joey cried. He ran up to Danny and pulled the tinsel out of his hair.

"Thank you," Danny said.

3

Joey placed one strand of tinsel on Danny's head. "It looks so much better when it's not in a big clump," Joey told Jesse.

"You're right." Jesse hurried over and looped a strand of tinsel over one of Danny's ears.

Michelle giggled. Jesse and Joey were always giving her dad a hard time. But they all really got along great.

Aunt Becky handed each of the twins a long piece of tinsel. "Go for it, guys!" she said. Nicky and Alex ran to the tree, stuck on their tinsel, and ran back to Becky for more strands.

Michelle, D.J., and Stephanie each grabbed some tinsel and joined in. Jesse climbed the ladder next to the tree and worked on the top.

"Perfect!" Danny announced.

"Okay, Dad. The tree's done. So where is the surprise?" Michelle demanded.

Ding-dong. The doorbell rang.

"I think your Christmas surprise has just arrived!" Danny told her.

"Yay! I'll get it!" Michelle raced to the front door. Comet, the family golden retriever, raced after her.

Michelle yanked open the door—and her mouth dropped open. Oh, no, she thought. This can't be my Christmas surprise. It can't be!

Chapter 2

♥ Danny rushed up behind her. "Here he is! The Tanner family Christmas surprise. Your cousin Marshall! He's spending the holidays with us!"

"Ho, ho, ho!" Marshall exclaimed.

Ho, ho, ho? Michelle rolled her eyes. *Ho-ho-horrible is more like it!* My Christmas is totally ruined, she thought. This is going to be the worst Christmas ever.

Michelle stared at her seven-year-old cousin. His light brown hair stuck out in all directions. He had spilled something— maybe ketchup—down the front of his sweater. He held a grubby paper bag in one hand. And his shoelaces were untied.

Marshall blew a big orange bubble-gum bubble. It popped on his face.

How could Marshall be our Christmas surprise? How could Dad do this to us? Marshall was a total pain. And he was a klutz. And all he talked about was bugs.

Kids who are bad all year should get Marshall for Christmas, Michelle thought. Not me! I've been really good. Well, pretty good.

Marshall's parents hurried up behind him. Marshall's dad carried a big suitcase. His mom held a cardboard box overflowing with Christmas presents.

"We can't stay," Marshall's dad said. He sounded out of breath. "Our flight leaves in an hour. Thanks so much for inviting Marshall to spend the holidays with you."

"We're glad to have him," Danny said. He took the suitcase and the box of presents and placed them in the hall.

"Have a good time, Marshall," his dad

said. He gave Marshall a hug. "We'll see you on Christmas Eve."

"Bye-bye. We'll miss you," Marshall's mom told him. She gave him a kiss. Then Marshall's parents ran back to the taxi waiting for them at the curb.

"Michelle, why don't you show Marshall our tree while I put this stuff away," Danny said. "Do you want me to take that paper bag, Marshall?"

Marshall hugged the big paper sack to his chest. "No, I'll keep this," he answered.

"Come on," Michelle said. She led Marshall into the living room.

"Marshall, it's great to see you!" Aunt Becky exclaimed.

"Come sit on the couch and try one of Dad's Christmas cupcakes," D.J. said. She handed him a chocolate cupcake with a Christmas tree made out of gumdrops on top.

Michelle hurried over to Stephanie. "Can you believe this is our surprise?" she whispered. "This is supposed to be Christmas—not April Fools'! Marshall is the most awful surprise ever!"

"Come on," Stephanie whispered back. "Be nice to him. Think how you'd feel if you had to spend your Christmas vacation away from home."

Stephanie headed for the kitchen. "You can't have a cupcake without milk, Marshall," Stephanie called over her shoulder. She came back with a big glass of milk. She handed it to Marshall.

"Thanks," Marshall said. Michelle watched him carefully as he took a drink. She waited for him to spill it. Marshall spills *everything*, she remembered. But he set the glass down carefully. He didn't spill any! she thought.

It's been a whole year since I've seen Marshall. Maybe he's changed, Michelle told herself. Maybe he doesn't spill things anymore. Maybe he doesn't even like bugs now!

"Hey, want to see something neato?" Marshall asked.

Michelle groaned. He still says *neato* though.

Marshall rummaged around in the big paper bag. He pulled out a long glass case.

"What's that?" Uncle Jesse asked.

"It's my ant farm!" Marshall said proudly. He placed it on the coffee table.

Uh-oh! He still likes bugs. Michelle let out a sigh.

"Ants are so cool. They can carry more than their own weight," Marshall said. "And you know what? There are some ants—they're called honeypot ants—they eat all this water and nectar. They get so big, they can't move. They just hang from the ceiling. And the other ants can feed off the honeypot ants. It's neato." Marshall talked about a zillion miles a minute.

"Wow, you really know a lot about ants," D.J. said.

"Yeah," Marshall answered. "And you

know what? I named one of my ants after Michelle!"

Yuck! Michelle thought. He named an ant after me? Gross!

"I don't get it," Joey said. He scratched his head. He looked really confused. "Michelle's not your aunt—she's your cousin!"

Joey cracked up. "Get it? She's not your *aunt!*"

"That's so lame," D.J. complained.

Marshall giggled. "Hey! There's Michelle. See? Right there!" He pointed to one of the ants.

Crash! The ant farm fell off the table.

Splash! Marshall's glass of milk tipped over.

"My ants!" Marshall jumped off the couch. He dropped his chocolate cupcake on the rug.

Comet lunged for the cupcake—and knocked into Michelle.

Michelle tumbled backward—into the Christmas tree!

"Are you okay?" Stephanie asked her.

Stephanie reached down and pulled Michelle to her feet.

Crunch.

"I'm fine," Michelle said. She looked down. "But the ballerina ornament isn't!"

Her favorite Christmas tree ornament lay shattered on the floor.

I knew it! Tears came to Michelle's eyes. This *is* going to be the worst Christmas ever!

Chapter 3

♥ No Cousin Marshall for the whole day! Michelle thought when she woke up the next morning. Yes!

She was going to the YMCA's Camp Yule Break from School. And that meant hours and hours with no Marshall!

Michelle pulled on her favorite red sweatshirt and her green polka-dot leggings. She felt very Christmassy.

Then she hurried downstairs for breakfast. Cassie Wilkins and Mandy Metz, her two best friends, would be there soon. They were going to the Y too!

I wish Lee was coming to camp with us, Michelle thought. He was one of their best friends at school. But Lee's Scout troop was having camp too, and he was going there.

The special program at the Y sounded great. There were all kinds of fun things to do—crafts, basketball, movies. Michelle couldn't wait.

Even with Cousin Marshall around, this will be a great week! Five fun days at camp, and then I have to wait only one more day for the best day of all—Christmas! Michelle thought.

She bounded into the kitchen. Her father hummed "Santa Claus Is Coming to Town" as he poured cranberry-nut pancake batter onto the sizzling griddle.

But something wasn't right. Marshall was the only one sitting at the table. Michelle sat down next to him. "Hi," she said.

"Hi," Marshall answered. "Want to hear

something neato?" He reached for his orange juice—and knocked it into his lap.

He reached for the napkins in the center of the table—and knocked over his bowl of cereal.

Danny ran over. "I'll clean that up," he said. "You go change your clothes, okay?"

"Okay." Marshall hurried out of the kitchen, dribbling juice behind him.

"Where is everybody?" Michelle asked.

"Gone," Danny said as he mopped up the orange juice. "Uncle Jesse's already left to take the twins to the dentist for a checkup. Then they're going to the mall to see Santa Claus. You should have seen the little guy's face. He was so excited!"

"Who?" Michelle asked. "Nicky or Alex?"

"Uncle Jesse!" Danny answered. "He said he was going to buy the boys some little Santa hats to wear in the picture!"

"That will be so cute!" Michelle said. "How about Stephanie and D.J.? Where are they?"

"D.J. already got a ride to the mall. Remember, she's wrapping presents at Milton's Department Store for the holidays to earn some extra money. She had to go in early for some training."

"I wish I could do that," Michelle said. She had a lot of presents to buy.

"And Stephanie's baby-sitting the Mitchell kids this week while their parents work."

Michelle knew her dad and Aunt Becky had to work all week too. She frowned. "So . . . what's Marshall doing?"

"Didn't I tell you?" Danny asked. "Marshall's going to camp with you."

"But, Dad—" Michelle began.

Marshall trotted back into the kitchen. "Do you think I can bring my ant farm to camp?" he asked.

"Welcome to the Camp Yule Break from School!" a tall woman with red hair called. "I'm Lauren, and I'm the head counselor this week."

"Her hair reminds me of a monarch butterfly," Marshall whispered. "It's almost the same color. And you know what? There are more than two hundred thousand kinds of butterflies and moths. And you know what?"

Michelle heard Cassie and Mandy start to giggle. She nudged Marshall. "Shhh!" she told him.

"We're going to have a lot of fun this week," Lauren went on. "We have lots of activities for you to choose from."

Lauren introduced all the other counselors. "We have only two rules this week," she added. "Be nice to your counselors and the other campers. And have a great time! Now Jeff and Catherine will tell you about some of the things you can do before lunch."

"What should we do?" Michelle asked when the counselors finished. Cassie wanted to play basketball. Mandy wanted to make gift wrap. Michelle wanted to do everything!

"How about we make gift wrap first, then go play basketball?" Michelle suggested.

"Neato!" Marshall cried.

"Uh, Marshall," Michelle said. "You don't have to hang around with me just because you're my cousin. Really. Hey, look—a bunch of the guys are going to play basketball. You'd probably rather go play with them, right? It's okay—you won't hurt my feelings."

Marshall shook his head. "I'd rather do whatever you're doing."

Cassie smiled at Michelle. "It's okay," she said.

"Come on!" Mandy exclaimed. "I want to make enough wrapping paper for all the presents I'm giving people."

She led the way over to a long table covered with newspaper. Scott and Mike, a couple of kids from Michelle's school, took the seats next to them.

"We're going to make potato stamp wrapping paper," Jeff told them. He was one of the counselors Lauren had introduced.

"First you draw a design on a sheet of paper. It has to be small enough to fit on a potato." Jeff held up a raw potato that had been cut in half.

"When you're finished, call me over, and I'll carve the design into the potato for you. Then you roll the potato in one of those trays of paint in front of you and use it to stamp your design on your wrapping paper."

"Cool!" Cassie said. She pulled a piece of paper in front of her. "I'm going to draw a little snowman."

"Will you pass me a pencil, Ladybug?" Marshall asked Michelle.

"Ladybug?" Mandy repeated.

"That's what I'm going to call Michelle," Marshall said. "Because ladybugs are the cutest bugs."

Michelle felt her face get hot. She didn't want to be called *Ladybug*. It sounded so stupid!

"And you know what?" Marshall asked. "Ladybugs are useful too. They eat aphids and other insects. People like to have them in their gardens."

Marshall picked up a pan of green paint. "I want to use this color," he said.

"Michelle eats bugs!" Scott called out.

"Michelle, will you come over to my house today?" Mike asked. "My mom is always complaining about the bugs on her flower bushes. Maybe you could eat some."

Everybody at the table started to laugh. Even Cassie and Mandy giggled.

"This is all your fault, Marshall!" Michelle wailed. "Everyone is laughing at me because of you."

Marshall spun toward her. The tray of paint wobbled in his hands.

"Nooo!" Michelle cried.

Chapter
4

♥ *Ker-splat!*

Marshall dropped the tray of paint in Michelle's lap.

The green paint flew up and splashed across her red sweatshirt. It spattered across her face. It soaked into her blond hair.

Everyone started laughing again. Even harder this time.

Michelle jumped up and raced to the bathroom. A few seconds later, Cassie and Mandy burst through the door.

"I hate Marshall!" Michelle exclaimed.

"He's totally ruining my Christmas vacation!"

"At least Marshall found someone else to eat with," Cassie said at lunchtime.

"Yeah, maybe he and that kid Pete will get to be friends," Mandy added.

"I hope so," Michelle said. "I don't think I can stand another minute with Marshall."

"Oh, he's not *that* bad," Mandy said as she pulled out her sandwich.

"Yeah, don't worry about it," Cassie agreed. "I've got a cousin like that too. Lucky for me, he lives in Canada."

"Is it okay if I sit here?" a girl with curly black hair asked.

"Sure," Michelle said. She noticed that the girl had painted half of her fingernails red and half green. And she had little jingle bell nail tattoos pasted on them.

"I love your fingernails!" Michelle told her.

"Want me to do yours?" the girl asked.

"I have some great reindeer nail tattoos and some red and green nail jewels. I'll do all three of you after we eat."

"Thanks! That would be so cool. I'm Michelle, and this is Cassie, and that's Mandy."

"I'm Alta Jacobson," the girl said.

Michelle opened her chicken salad sandwich and fruit salad. Her dad made the best lunches. He had even packed home-baked cookies for dessert.

Alta opened her lunch bag and frowned. "Yuck. What's this supposed to be?"

Michelle glanced over. Alta held a pink plastic container filled with a bunch of leftovers all mixed together.

"That fruit salad of yours looks delicious!" Alta said. "Want to trade?"

"Uh, not really," Michelle said.

Alta laughed. "I don't blame you!"

"How about if I split the fruit salad with you?" Michelle asked. She dumped part of the salad on a napkin and pushed it toward Alta.

"And you can have half my sandwich," Mandy said.

"And some of my celery and carrots." Cassie tossed her a plastic bag of vegetables.

"That's so sweet of you guys!" Alta exclaimed, her blue eyes shining. "Hey, I'm having a Christmas party on Friday. Do you want to come?"

"A Christmas party—cool!" Michelle cried.

"My parents are renting a bus and taking everyone to Santa's Playland," Alta told them.

"Oh, I've heard of that place!" Michelle said. "It's in Santa Cruz, right?"

"Yeah. And they have real live reindeer," Alta answered. "And all kinds of rides. There's this amazing Christmas tree ride, where you sit in giant ornaments. They go up and down and spin around."

"I'd love to see a reindeer up close," Cassie said.

"It sounds awesome! Thanks for inviting us," Michelle exclaimed.

"Ladybug! Ladybug!" Marshall yelled from across the room. Then he ran toward Michelle. Can I just pretend I don't know him? Michelle thought.

Alta's eyes opened wide. "Who's that?" she asked.

Michelle sighed. "It's my cousin Marshall," she admitted. "He's staying with us over Christmas vacation."

He skidded to a stop in front of Michelle. "Ladybug, look! It's a daddy longlegs." Marshall leaned over and opened his cupped hands.

"A spider!" Alta cried. "Get it away from me!"

"Daddy longlegs aren't really spiders. They just look like spiders," Marshall said. "And you know what? You can pull off one of a daddy longlegs's legs and it will still be okay. And—"

"Get it away!" Alta slapped at Marshall's hand.

The daddy longlegs flew off—and landed in Alta's fruit salad.

Alta jumped up. Her chair fell over with a *thump.*

Marshall calmly reached over and caught the daddy longlegs. He held it trapped in his hands.

"That was so gross!" Alta said.

"I'm sorry, Ladybug," Marshall whispered. "I'll take it away." He ran back across the room.

Alta stared after Marshall with a disgusted look on her face. *"You* can come to my party, Michelle," Alta said. "But leave your cousin at home!"

Chapter 5

♥ "Did you all have fun at your first day of camp?" Mandy's mother asked when she picked them up.

"It was neato!" Marshall answered.

Neato. Michelle rolled her eyes at Cassie and Mandy. They tried not to laugh.

Michelle bounced up and down in her seat. She couldn't wait to get home. She wanted to tell her dad all about Alta's amazing Christmas party and ask him if she could go.

Mrs. Metz pulled up in front of Michelle's house. Michelle and Marshall climbed out of the car. "See you later," Michelle called to Cassie and Mandy. "Thanks for the ride, Mrs. Metz."

Michelle hurried into the house with Marshall right behind her. "Why don't you go check on your ants?" Michelle asked him. "I bet they missed you. Tell the Michelle ant I said hi."

Marshall grinned at her. "I'll be back in a minute," he said.

That doesn't give me much time, Michelle thought. She couldn't talk to her dad about the party with Marshall around.

"Dad?" she called. "Where are you?"

"In the living room," Danny answered.

Michelle rushed into the living room and plopped down on the sofa next to him. "What happened to you?" he exclaimed. He pointed at the paint stains on her sweatshirt.

"Marshall happened to me," Michelle answered. "He spills everything he touches!"

"He's going to be here a week. I'd better buy an extra-large bottle of stain remover next time I'm at the store," Danny said.

"Yeah," Michelle agreed. She didn't have much time left. Marshall would probably find her in a few more seconds.

"Dad, I met this really cool girl at camp," Michelle said as fast as she could. "Her name is Alta Jacobson."

"Isn't that something," Danny said. "I know her father, Richard. We worked together on that community fund-raising committee last year."

"That's great," Michelle said. "Alta invited me and Cassie and Mandy to a Christmas party at Santa's Playland! It will be so much fun. There's a Santa's-sleigh roller-coaster ride and live reindeer that you can pet and tons of other cool stuff! Can I go?"

"Sure, honey," Danny said. "It sounds like you'll have a great time."

"Thanks, Dad!" Michelle jumped up and ran toward the stairs. She had to call

Cassie and Mandy right away and find out if their parents said they could go to the party.

"I'm sure she wouldn't mind if Marshall comes too," Danny called after her.

Michelle spun around and stared at her father. "But, Dad!" she exclaimed. "Alta didn't invite him."

"I'm sure she will if you explain the situation," he said.

Michelle lowered her voice. "I don't think Alta likes Marshall very much. He dropped a spider on her lunch."

"It was an accident, wasn't it?" Danny asked.

Michelle nodded.

"I'm sure Alta realizes that now," Danny told her.

"Maybe," Michelle mumbled. "But couldn't Marshall stay here and play with the twins? That's fun. I love playing with them."

"Come on, Michelle," her dad said. "If you had to choose between riding on a

Santa's-sleigh roller coaster or coloring with the twins, which would you pick?"

"Nicky and Alex have this great coloring book. The pages are as big as posters. . . ." Michelle sighed. "Okay, I would pick the roller coaster," she admitted.

"Me too," Danny answered. "The twins chew on their crayons. They're always all slimy."

Michelle laughed.

"Talk to Alta," her dad said. "I'm sure she knows how it is when you have company. You can't leave your guest at home."

"I'll talk to her," Michelle agreed.

But I bet it's not going to work, she thought.

Chapter
6

♥ *Sluuurp!*

"Michelle, what is your cousin doing?" Alta asked at lunch the next day.

Michelle glanced over at Marshall. He had taken a bite out of his apple. He had his mouth pressed over the hole—and was sucking the juice out.

Sluuurp!

"Marshall, what are you doing?" Michelle asked.

"Huh?" Marshall raised his head, and apple juice dribbled down his chin.

"What are you *doing?*" Michelle repeated.

"Oh. I'm trying to eat like a bloodsucking fly," Marshall answered.

"Ewww!" Alta exclaimed.

"They tear open a piece of skin—like on a monkey—then they suck the blood up. Isn't that cool? And you know what?"

Alta stood up. "I'm leaving," she announced. "I can't listen to this gross stuff while I eat. See you guys later."

"Marshall, I think I hear Pete calling you," Michelle said.

"Really?" Marshall asked.

"Yeah. Why don't you go find him. He'd probably like to see you eat like a bloodsucking fly!" Michelle said.

"Okay." Marshall picked up his apple and started across the room. "Pete?" he yelled. "Where are you?"

"I had to get rid of him for a minute," Michelle told Cassie and Mandy. "I have a major problem."

"What's wrong?" Cassie asked.

"My dad wants me to ask Alta if Marshall can come to her party," Michelle said. "He won't let me go without Marshall."

"Oh, no!" Mandy moaned. "You have to go to the party, Michelle. You have to! It's going to be fantastic."

"I know! It will be the best Christmas party ever. I can't miss it." Michelle shook her head. "But Alta thinks Marshall is gross. She can't even stand to eat lunch with him. She's not going to want him at her party. What am I going to do?"

Marshall ran back up and sat next to Michelle. "I couldn't find Pete," he said.

"That's too bad," Michelle answered. Too bad for me, she added to herself.

"Alta's pretty cool," Cassie said. "Maybe she'll understand your . . . problem."

"What problem?" Marshall asked. He brought his apple up to his mouth and took a big slurp.

"No problem," Michelle said quickly. "I just need to talk to Alta for a second." She stood up.

Marshall stood up. "I'll come too!" he cried.

"Marshall, stay with us," Mandy said. "Cassie and I want to do a report about beetles for school. Do you know anything about them?"

Marshall sat back down. "Sure. There is this one beetle, it's called Goliath. It's six inches long. And you know what?"

Michelle smiled at Mandy. Good one! she thought. Marshall can talk about bugs for hours.

Now I just have to find Alta. Michelle stared around the room and spotted Alta at a table near the windows. She hurried over.

"Uh, hi," Michelle said.

"Sorry I had to leave before," Alta told her. "What your cousin was doing with that apple was *sooo* gross. How can you stand him?"

"He's not so bad," Michelle answered. "I wanted to tell you that I can go to your party."

35

"Great!" Alta exclaimed.

"There's just one problem," Michelle said.

"What?" Alta asked.

"I can only go if . . ." Michelle swallowed hard.

"What?" Alta asked again.

"I can only go if my cousin Marshall can go too," Michelle blurted out.

"No way!" Alta squealed. "That would totally ruin my party! I'm sorry, Michelle. But if you have to bring your cousin, you are officially *un*invited!"

Chapter
7

♥ Marshall pounded on the bathroom door. "Michelle, do you want to play with my ant farm?" he yelled.

Michelle sighed. The second she got home from camp she ran into the bathroom and locked the door. She thought that would give her at least a couple of minutes away from her cousin.

Marshall thumped on the door again. "Michelle?" he called.

I guess not, Michelle thought. I guess there is no place in the whole universe I can go to get away from Marshall.

"Marshall, I'm taking a bath!" Michelle exclaimed. She filled the sink with water and made splashing noises.

"You're taking a bath now?" he asked.

"Yes!" Michelle splashed even harder. "I'm going to wash my hair. I won't be able to hear you with the soap in my ears!"

"Okay," Marshall said. "We can play with the ant farm when you get out. The Michelle ant says hi."

Michelle heard Marshall's footsteps heading away from the door. Yes! she thought. Finally!

She sat down on the edge of the tub. Okay, she thought. I can't miss Alta's party. That would ruin my whole Christmas. So I have to find something else for Marshall to do on Friday. Something fun, so he won't feel bad about missing Alta's party.

I know! Dad's making his special Christmas gingerbread house on Friday. Marshall could help him!

Michelle darted out of the bathroom and rushed down the stairs to the kitchen.

"How was camp?" her father asked. He cracked an egg into a mixing bowl.

"Fine," Michelle answered. "Do you know what Marshall loves even more than bugs?" she asked.

Danny cracked another egg into the bowl. "No, what?"

Michelle crossed her fingers behind her back. "Food," she answered.

It's not a big lie, she thought. And it's an important part of my plan to go to Alta's party!

"Really?" Danny said, stirring the batter. "Marshall?"

"Umm-hmm. And he thinks you're a *wonderful* cook," Michelle told him.

Danny smiled. "Isn't that sweet."

"Yeah, Marshall is sweet," she forced herself to say. Then she shook her head and gave a big sigh. "Poor guy."

Danny stopped stirring. His face wrinkled into a worried frown. "Poor guy?

Michelle, has something happened to Marshall?"

"He's fine, Dad," Michelle said quickly. "I just think—well, I think he's probably bored just hanging out with me and my friends. You know, because we're girls. I think he wishes he could hang out with a guy. You know, someone cool."

Michelle cleared her throat. "Like you."

"Me?" Danny said, surprised.

Ding! The timer on the stove rang. Danny took a small bowl of melted chocolate out of the microwave. "Oh, I'm sure Marshall is having a good time with you. He would rather spend time with someone his own age than with me."

Darn, Michelle thought. This isn't working.

"No, really, Dad!" Michelle insisted. "I'm sure he'd like to hang out and cook with you—but I think he's too shy to ask."

Danny stirred the chocolate into the big mixing bowl. "Well, you know, I could use some help with all my holiday baking."

"Yeah, especially when you make that

gingerbread house on Friday. That's a big job. I know! You should give Marshall some lessons!" Michelle suggested. "You always say cooking is a science. Right? And Marshall's good at science."

"Well, I'd be glad to give him some lessons," Danny said as he poured his batter into some pans. "If you're sure he'd enjoy it."

"Wait here!" Michelle said. "I'll go get him."

Michelle ran to the laundry room where Marshall kept his ant farm.

"Michelle the ant says to tell you you're neato," Marshall said.

"Great," Michelle answered. "You know, Marshall, my dad really likes you."

"Really?" Marshall smiled. "I like him too. He's nice."

"And you know what?" Michelle went on. "I think he'd really like it if you helped him bake stuff for Christmas. But he's too shy to ask."

"I didn't know Uncle Danny was shy," Marshall said.

"Oh, he is," Michelle said. "He just doesn't show it. So—want to learn how to cook?"

"Sure," Marshall said. "When?"

"Now—come on!" She dragged her cousin into the kitchen. "Marshall's here for his cooking lessons!"

"Great!" Danny said. "Here's an apron."

Yes! My plan is working! Michelle thought.

"Well, I'll see you two later. Have fun!" Michelle headed out of the kitchen.

"Ladybug, wait!" Marshall cried. "Where are you going?"

"Uh, don't worry about me," Michelle said. "I'll find something to do."

"I don't want to cook if you're not going to cook," Marshall said.

Chapter

8

♥ "But, no, I—" Michelle began.

"Come on, Michelle," her father said.
"It'll be fun. Now, first you need to wash
your hands with soap."

Michelle put on her apron and washed
her hands. Oh, well. She always liked
helping her dad with the holiday baking.
And if Marshall had a good time this afternoon, he would probably want to help her
dad on Friday—even if Michelle *wasn't*
around.

"Why don't you cut out some Christmas
cookies? Then after they bake, you can

decorate them," Danny said. "The dough is in the fridge."

Christmas cookies! Michelle loved to decorate Christmas cookies. She loved to eat them too!

Michelle took the chilled dough out of the refrigerator. She dragged a big box of cookie cutters from the cabinet. She set out colored sugar, sprinkles, icing, and other decorations. Then she rolled out the dough.

"I'm going to make angels first," Michelle said. She cut out several angels and carefully placed them on the baking sheet. "What about you, Marshall?"

Marshall dug through the cookie cutters. "This looks good!"

"But Marshall," Michelle protested. "That's not a *Christmas* cookie cutter. That's an *Easter* egg!"

"That's okay," Marshall said. "Just wait."

When they had filled a tray with cookies, Danny popped it in the oven. They kept working until they had filled ten trays. Michelle's family always gave cookies as holiday presents, and they liked to hang some on their Christmas tree too.

"Now comes the really fun part—decorating!" Michelle told Marshall.

Michelle started work on one of her angel cookies. I'll give her a blue dress with little silver balls on it, she decided.

She and Marshall worked in silence. About an hour later, Danny wandered over. "Um, Marshall . . . what exactly are those?" he asked.

"Insects! This one's a ladybug. It's for Michelle." Marshall smiled at her. "This one's a tick. That one's a dung beetle. And here's a spittlebug, a stinkbug, and an American cockroach. Don't they look neato?"

Danny rubbed his forehead. "Very . . . creative, Marshall."

Very *gross!* Michelle thought. The ladybug *was* kind of cute. But who would want to eat a cockroach Christmas cookie?

"I think I'll take these to Y camp," Marshall said proudly. "I bet Pete would like one. And Cassie, and Mandy, and that girl Alta—"

"No!" Michelle shrieked. "I mean, uh, maybe you should save them and . . . and give them to your parents!"

"Excellent idea!" Danny quickly agreed. "I'll find you a nice tin for them. Now we'd better clean up so I can start dinner."

"What are we cooking tonight, Uncle Danny?" Marshall asked. "Michelle and I want to help too. Right, Ladybug?"

"Marshall and Michelle helped me cook tonight," Danny told the family when they sat down to dinner.

"Um, it looks . . . very interesting," Aunt Becky said politely, and took a bite.

"What is it?" D.J. asked. She poked at the food on her plate.

"Well, I got the idea from one of my insect books," Marshall said. "Did you know people in Africa eat sautéed beetles?"

46

Joey froze with his fork halfway to his mouth.

"Ewwww!" Alex shrieked. He spit out his food.

"Marshall!" Stephanie gasped. "Does this have sautéed beetles in it?"

"Calm down, everybody," Danny hollered. "There are no sautéed beetles in this dinner—I promise!"

"So what is it, then?" Uncle Jesse demanded. "I'm not eating another bite until I know what this is."

"It's just vegetables in cheese sauce," Danny said.

"I just chopped up the vegetables into tiny pieces first, then sautéed them," Marshall said. "I guess I burned some of them."

Michelle didn't feel like eating. She kept thinking about bugs. She noticed no one else was eating either.

Except Marshall. "Hey, it's still pretty good!" he declared. "Cooking is fun. What

47

are we going to make tomorrow night, Uncle Danny?"

"Take-out pizza!" Joey blurted out.

"We, uh, always have take-out pizza on Thursday night," Aunt Becky added. "Right, guys?"

"Right!" everyone agreed.

"But tomorrow night is Wednesday," Marshall said.

"I meant Wednesday," Aunt Becky said.

"Right!" everyone agreed again.

Rats! Michelle thought. My Cooking with Uncle Danny plan just went down the garbage disposal. Nobody's going to want to eat the gingerbread house if Marshall helps make it.

I have to think of something else—and fast!

Chapter
9

♥ "Do you know what Marshall loves more than bugs?" Michelle asked Joey. It was their turn to clean up after dinner.

Joey wrinkled his nose as he scraped a plateful of Marshall's special vegetables and cheese into the garbage. "What?" he asked.

Michelle crossed her fingers behind her back. "Jokes," she lied. "And he thinks you're really funny. He wants to be a comedian like you someday."

I hope this works better than it did with Dad, Michelle thought. Maybe Joey and

Marshall will have fun together—and Joey will want to do something with Marshall on Friday.

"I bet Marshall would really like you to teach him some jokes," Michelle continued. "But I think he's too shy to ask."

As soon as the dishes were done, Michelle and Joey went looking for Marshall. They found him in the living room, reading a volume of the encyclopedia.

The letter *I*, Michelle noticed. That figures. I—for *i*nsects.

"Hey, Marshall," Joey asked. "How would you like to do a comedy act with me at a Christmas party on Friday?"

Friday? Michelle thought. This is super perfect. Alta's party is on Friday!

"Really?" Marshall said. "That sounds neato."

"Great!" Joey said. "Come on downstairs and let's get to work."

But Marshall grabbed Michelle's arm. "Only if Michelle comes too, though."

"No, really," Michelle said. "You don't want me—"

"Sure we do, Michelle," Joey said. "Come on. You can help us practice our lines."

Oh, no! It happened again! Michelle thought. I wish Marshall would agree to do *something* without me! She slowly followed Joey and Marshall downstairs.

Joey ran over to his bookshelf. He stared thoughtfully at a row of black binders. Finally he pulled one out.

"What's that?" Michelle asked.

"I have a copy of almost every comedy routine I've ever done," Joey said. "They come in handy when I need some funny material fast."

He flipped through some pages. He stopped and read a few lines and chuckled. "This is pretty funny. Let's try this one."

Joey handed Marshall a sheet of paper. Marshall read the first joke. "A duck walked into a drugstore one cold Christmas Eve and said, 'Give me some Chap Stick and put it on my bill.' "

Michelle cracked up.

"I don't get it," Marshall said.

"A bill is what you owe on something you buy," Joey explained. "And a duck has a bill. And since a duck doesn't have lips, he'd put Chap Stick on his bill. Get it?"

"Oh, yeah." Marshall grinned. "Neato! Let's do some more."

They practiced about an hour. Michelle was getting worried. She had to explain half the jokes to Marshall. And he had a hard time memorizing his lines.

"Maybe we should try this stuff out on an audience," Joey suggested.

"Are you kidding?" Michelle exclaimed. "I mean—so soon?"

"Just the rest of the family," Joey said. "Sometimes I have to do my act in front of people before it starts working the way I want it to."

Joey led the way up to the living room.

Danny, Aunt Becky, Uncle Jesse, and Stephanie were watching TV together. Joey snapped the set off.

"Hey!" Stephanie protested. "We were watching that."

Joey ignored her. "Hello, everybody," he began. "We're Joey and Marshall, and we're here to put a little Christmas cheer in your stockings. So just sit back and enjoy the show. Take it away, Marshall!"

Michelle sat down on the couch next to Stephanie. Marshall waved at everybody. Then he cleared his throat and glanced nervously at Joey.

Joey smiled and nodded.

"Okay," Marshall said. "A chicken walked into a store—"

"Duck!" Michelle whispered loudly.

"Huh?" Marshall said.

Michelle rolled her eyes. She jumped up and ran over to her cousin. "A duck!" she whispered in his ear. "It was a duck, not a chicken!" Michelle rushed back to her seat.

"Oops! Okay, let me start over. A duck, not a chicken, walked into a store. It was a . . . wait a minute, let me think. A grocery store?" He looked at Joey.

Joey shook his head. "A drugstore!" he reminded Marshall.

"Oh, yeah. A drugstore," Marshall repeated. "Anyway, the duck walked into the drugstore and asked the drugstore person, 'Do you have—' "

Marshall stopped and stared at the ground. "Oh, wait a minute. I forgot to tell you! This happened on Christmas Eve."

Michelle glanced around at her family. At least they're being polite, she thought. No one has started booing or anything.

" 'So, anyway,' the duck says, 'do you have anything for chapped lips?' I mean, the duck says, 'Do you have any Chap Stick?' 'Yes, here's some right here,' the store guy said."

Marshall cracked up. He laughed until he snorted. "This is really funny."

Doesn't he notice he's the only one laughing? Michelle wondered.

"So, the duck said, 'Thanks.' " Marshall looked proud of himself for finishing the joke.

Michelle shook her head. "No," she mouthed at him. "That's not the way the joke goes."

"Oh! I almost forgot! And then the duck said, 'Charge it!' "

Nobody laughed.

"I don't get it," Uncle Jesse whispered loudly.

Aunt Becky jabbed him in the ribs. "Shhh!"

Joey rubbed his hands over his face. "Marshall, come here."

Marshall shuffled over. "What?"

Joey whispered in his ear.

"Oh!" Marshall exclaimed. " 'Put it on my bill!' That's what the duck said. Get it?" he asked.

"You've been a great audience, everyone. Thanks for listening," Joey said.

"But we have more jokes," Marshall reminded him.

"Let's save some for later," Joey answered.

"So, Joey," Marshall asked. "What time is the big show on Friday?"

"Well, uh—" Joey turned red. "You know, gosh, I just remembered something. The job lasts till midnight, and that's, uh, way past your bedtime. So, uh, it's really been fun, Marshall, but I guess we have to forget about Friday night."

What a disaster! Michelle thought. Cooking with Dad is out. Comedy with Joey is out. I need another plan—fast!

But first I have to get through another day at camp with Marshall.

Chapter

10

♥   "Anyone want a piece of my Orange Blaster gum?" Marshall asked at Y camp the next day. "It's super sour. It makes your tongue hurt."

"Uh, no thanks," Mandy answered.

Michelle shook her head.

"Hey, Marshall," Cassie said. "Somebody said Pete was looking for you."

"Really?" Marshall asked. "Where is he?"

"I don't know," Cassie said. "Maybe in the gym."

Marshall ran off to find his friend. Cassie giggled.

"Cassie!" Michelle said. "Was that the truth?"

"No! I just made it up," Cassie replied with a grin. "He'll find Pete and they'll hang out and everything will be fine."

"Yeah, you're right," Michelle said. "Come on, I want to make one of those stained glass Christmas tree ornaments." She led the way over to the craft table.

"Hi, girls," Catherine called. Michelle smiled at the counselor.

"Sit down, and I'll get you started on your ornaments," Catherine said. "Just pick one of these metal frames, set it on a tray, and fill it with some of these plastic beads—whatever colors you want. Then call me over. I'll stick a piece of wax paper over the whole thing and iron it. The beads will melt—and your ornament will be done!"

Michelle decided to make a rainbow-colored star. Mandy began a blue and green heart. Cassie wanted to try to make a yellow and red peace symbol.

"Have you found something for Marshall to do on Friday?" Cassie asked.

"No, not yet. And it's only two days until the party!" Michelle answered.

"Maybe Alta will change her mind," Mandy said. "Maybe she'll say it's okay for Marshall to come."

"Yeah," Cassie added. "Marshall's not so awful."

"Hey, Michelle! Hi, Cassie! Hi, Mandy!" Michelle looked up. Alta ran over to them. She made a jingling sound with every step. Michelle noticed she had little bells looped through the laces on her tennis shoes. How cute, Michelle thought.

Alta sat down across the table from Michelle. "I want to make one of these ornaments too." She picked a metal frame shaped like a Christmas tree and started filling it with beads.

Marshall ran up to the table. He stood behind Alta, chomping on his Orange Blaster bubble gum.

"Pete couldn't have been looking for

me," he told Cassie. "Lauren said Pete stayed home today. He has the flu."

"Oh, uh, I guess it was someone else," Cassie mumbled.

"That tree ornament is neato!" Marshall exclaimed. He leaned over Alta to get a closer look.

Plop!

His wad of Orange Blaster gum fell out of his mouth—and landed in Alta's black hair.

No! Michelle thought. Oh, no!

"What did you do?" Alta shrieked. She reached up and felt the wad of gum in her hair.

"I'll get it out!" Michelle jumped up and raced around the table to Alta. She grabbed the gum and pulled.

It stretched and stretched. But it stayed stuck in Alta's hair.

"You're hurting me!" Alta cried.

Catherine ran up to them. "What happened?" she exclaimed.

"Marshall put gum in my hair!" Alta yelled.

"I . . . I . . ." Marshall stared at Alta's head with his mouth hanging open.

"It was an accident," Michelle explained.

"Let me take a look," Catherine said. She gently ran her fingers through Alta's hair. "Maybe we can cut it out."

Alta glared at Marshall. "Stay away from me!" she yelled. "I don't want you to talk to me. I don't want you to sit at the same table with me. I don't even want you to *look* at me! Just stay away!"

Chapter
11

♥ "Michelle, Michelle, where are you?" Marshall called.

Michelle sat absolutely still in the hall closet. She needed time to think. Without Marshall around!

I've got to find something for him to do on Friday, she thought. Alta is never going to change her mind about him. Never!

Not after what he did to her today. She had one clump of hair that was a whole lot shorter than the rest. It was where Catherine cut out the gum.

Think, Michelle ordered herself. Cooking with Dad is out. A comedy show with Joey is out. Dad already said Marshall couldn't hang out with the twins. D.J. has to work.

That left Steph, Aunt Becky, and Uncle Jesse. Maybe one of them could take Marshall someplace on Friday.

Michelle opened the closet door halfway and stuck her head out. She looked both ways. No Marshall.

She ran up the stairs to her room as fast as she could. Stephanie lay sprawled on her bed with her headphones on.

Michelle hurried over and pulled them off.

"Hey!" Stephanie cried.

"Steph, Marshall really likes you," Michelle told her. "He'd really like to hang out with you. He's tired of being with girls all the time," Michelle said.

Stephanie laughed. "And what am I—a goldfish?"

Oops! "I mean, he'd like to hang around

with someone older," Michelle said quickly. "Someone cool, someone—"

"Michelle, I'm spending half my Christmas vacation baby-sitting already. Besides, aren't *you* supposed to be entertaining Marshall?" Stephanie asked.

"Yeah," Michelle muttered.

She hurried out of the room and up to Uncle Jesse and Aunt Becky's apartment on the third floor. Michelle had to work fast. She was sure Marshall would track her down any second.

Michelle burst through the door to the third floor. "Hi, Michelle," Aunt Becky said. "You're just in time to see the twins in their costumes for their preschool's Christmas pageant."

Nicky and Alex were both dressed up like reindeer. They were so cute. I've hardly had any time to spend with the twins since Marshall got here, Michelle realized.

Nicky jumped up and down—and his

antlers flew off. "I'm Dancer!" he announced proudly.

"I guess we need tighter elastic," Aunt Becky said. She picked up the antlers from the floor.

"Guess who I am, Michelle," Alex said.

"Um, the Easter bunny," she teased. "Or wait, I know, the tooth fairy."

"No, no, no!" Alex shook his head so hard, *his* antlers flew off. "I'm Rudolph."

"Oh, that's why your nose is red," Michelle said. "I thought you had a bad cold."

"I have to remember to buy film," Aunt Becky said. "I want to take a ton of pictures Friday afternoon."

Uh-oh, Michelle thought. "Friday afternoon?" she repeated.

"That's when the play is," Aunt Becky said.

Uncle Jesse will be at the play too, Michelle realized. Maybe they could take Marshall with them. "I bet Marshall would love to see that play," Michelle said.

"I wish you all could come," Aunt Becky answered. "But each family gets only two tickets."

This is horrible. Who else can I get to do something with Marshall? Michelle thought. There's no one left.

Wait. There is *one* more person, she thought. Lee! Lee was one of her best friends from school. He would help her!

"See you guys later. You look great!" Michelle called. She raced down the stairs to the phone in the hallway outside her room. She dialed Lee's number.

"Lee, how would you like to trade lunches every day in January?" Michelle asked the second he picked up the phone. She didn't even bother to say hello.

"That would be great!" Lee answered.

I knew he'd say that, Michelle thought. Lee loved Danny's lunches more than anything. He was always trying to get her to trade with him.

"What do I have to do?" he asked.

"Just invite my cousin Marshall over,"

Michelle told him. She twisted the phone cord around her finger. Please say yes, she thought.

"What's wrong with him?" Lee asked.

"Nothing!" Michelle promised.

"Come on, Michelle," Lee said.

"Okay, okay," Michelle said. "He really likes bugs. That's practically all he talks about. And he's sort of a klutz. He'll probably spill stuff on you. And the way he eats is sort of weird sometimes. But that's it."

"I'll do it—if you throw in some of your dad's Christmas cookies."

"Deal!" Michelle cried.

"So when should I invite him over?" Lee asked.

"Friday," Michelle answered. She did a little victory dance by the phone table.

"Oh, man! I can't," Lee said.

"Why?" Michelle wailed.

"I have to go to my sister's ballet recital. *The Nutcracker* or something," Lee explained.

"Take him with you," she begged.

"I can't. Hang on. My mom needs to use the phone. I've got to go. Merry Christmas!"

Michelle hung up the phone. She slumped down on the floor and buried her head in her hands. Merry Christmas, she thought. Yeah, right!

Michelle heard footsteps coming up the stairs and down the hall. They stopped in front of her. "What's wrong, Michelle?"

Michelle uncovered her face and looked up. Marshall stood there with his ant farm in his arms.

"You!" she answered. "You have ruined my whole Christmas, Marshall!"

Marshall's green eyes grew wide. "How? What did I do wrong?"

"Everything!"

"Just tell me what I did," Marshall begged. "I promise I won't do it again."

"Really?" Michelle asked.

"I promise," Marshall repeated.

"Wait here." Michelle rushed into her

room. She grabbed a big sheet of construction paper and a purple marker. Then she hurried back to Marshall. She sat down on the floor and started to write.

"What are you doing?" Marshall asked.

"I'm making a list," Michelle explained. "Of all the things you're going to promise not to do when you're around me. Then you have to sign it."

"Okay," Marshall agreed.

"Rule number one," Michelle said as she wrote. "Never mention bugs."

"But, Michelle, that's my favorite—"

"Fine, forget it." Michelle started to rip the construction paper in half.

Marshall grabbed her arm. "Okay, Ladybug. I—I promise."

"Rule number two," Michelle said. "Quit calling me Ladybug!"

"But—"

"I mean it!" Michelle said.

"Rule number three: Stop saying *neato* all the time. Rule number four . . ." Michelle bit her pen, thinking. "Don't eat

like a bloodsucking fly—or any other insect. Rule number five: Stop spilling
things. Rule number six: Watch where
you're going. Rule number seven: Quit
hanging all over me. You have to stay at
least three feet away. . . ."

Michelle kept going till she had nine
rules. She thought for a moment, then
wrote down one more. "Rule number ten:
Make Alta like you."

She handed Marshall her pen. "Here,
sign it."

Marshall stared at her for a minute.
"Okay, Michelle," he said. "If that's what
you really want. . . ."

Michelle watched him scrawl his name
on the paper. Maybe this will work, she
thought. Maybe when Alta sees how dif-
ferent Marshall is, she won't mind if he
comes to her party.

Maybe my Christmas is saved!

Chapter

12

♥ "I have to find Alta," Marshall said. He headed into the Y. He walked super slow. He kept his eyes glued to his feet.

"Why is Marshall walking like that?" Cassie asked. She and Mandy and Michelle followed Marshall inside.

"I made a list of rules for Marshall," Michelle explained. "He's following rule number six. That one is *Watch where you're going.*"

"Why does he want to find Alta?" Mandy said.

"Probably for rule number ten. That's *Make Alta like you.*"

"Tough rule," Cassie commented.

"Yeah," Michelle agreed. "I hope he can do it. Let's go with him. I want to be there if he makes a mistake."

Michelle felt her stomach flip-flop as they followed Marshall across the basketball court. Alta sat in the bleachers, waiting for a game to start up.

Marshall stared at Alta. "Um, hi," he said. "Um . . ."

Michelle jumped in. "Marshall promised me he wouldn't talk about bugs anymore," she told Alta. "And he's going to eat the normal way, and not spill anything. Can't you give him another chance?"

Alta studied Marshall. "I'll do anything you want," he promised her.

"Hmmm. I'll think about it," Alta said. "While I'm making up my mind, would you do me a favor? Go get me an orange juice from the snack table."

"I can handle that," Marshall said. He slowly made his way across the gym.

"Don't take all day, please," Alta called after him. Marshall picked up his speed.

Michelle, Cassie, and Mandy sat down in the bleachers next to Alta. "Great hat," Cassie said.

Michelle glared at her. Didn't she know Alta was only wearing the hat to cover up the spot where they cut her hair?

Cassie blushed. "Oops," she mumbled.

"Michelle," Alta said. "Do you want me to do your nails again? I have some really cool silver and gold polish. And some cute nail tattoos that look like little red bows."

She doesn't sound mad at me. Cool! "That would be great!" Michelle exclaimed.

A few minutes later, Marshall returned with Alta's juice. He handed it to her very, very carefully. "Here you go!"

Michelle smiled at him. "Good job!"

Alta stared at the cup of juice. "Oh, Marshall," she said sweetly. "You got me orange juice and I asked for grape juice." She handed the cup back to him. "I can't drink this. Orange juice gives me a rash."

"But—" Michelle began.

"No problem," Marshall interrupted her. "I'll drink the orange juice. I'll go get your grape juice right now."

Alta reached into her bag and pulled out two bottles of nail polish. She handed Mandy a bottle of gold polish. "Why don't you do Cassie's nails while I do Michelle's," she said.

"Great. Thanks," Cassie answered.

Alta unscrewed the top of the silver polish. "Hold out your hand," she told Michelle.

"What an awesome color!" Michelle exclaimed.

Marshall came up with Alta's grape juice cradled in both hands. He handed it to her without spilling a drop.

"Hey, Marshall," Alta said. "I want to try some green and red glitter on my nails. Would you get me some from the craft table?"

"Sure," Marshall said. "I'll be right back."

"You know what, Michelle?" Alta said when he was gone. "Your cousin is kind of useful to have around."

"I guess so," Michelle said. She watched Alta stroke on the shiny polish. She loved the way it glistened.

Marshall arrived with the glitter. "Thanks," Alta said.

Alta doesn't mind having Marshall around anymore, Michelle thought. I bet she's going to let him come to her party. And I'll be *re*invited!

Chapter

13

♥ "Marshall, will you trade with me?" Alta asked at lunch.

Marshall stared at Alta's pink plastic container full of leftover Chinese food. His nose wrinkled. "Uncle Danny made my favorite lunch today. Tuna salad with apples."

"Oh." Alta frowned. "I thought you meant it when you said you would do *anything,* but—"

"I did! I did!" Marshall slid his sandwich over to Alta.

Whew! I thought Marshall was going to

blow it! Michelle watched her cousin take a tiny bite of the cold rice and vegetables. She thought he was going to gag. But he swallowed it.

Marshall reached into his lunch bag and pulled out one of the sugar cookies he and Michelle made. He raised it to his mouth.

"Hey! That's my cookie!" Alta reached over and snatched it out of his hand. "We traded lunches. That means I get everything you brought. And you get everything I brought."

"What else do you have?" Marshall asked.

"That's it." Alta pointed to the plastic container.

"I'm not very hungry anyway," Marshall mumbled.

"Marshall, my shoe came untied. Will you tie it for me?" Alta asked.

Marshall glanced at Michelle. Then he hurried over to Alta. He sat down on the floor next to her and tied her sneaker.

Then he stood up and started back toward his chair.

"Can you make a double knot? Please?" Alta asked.

Marshall nodded and returned to Alta. Should I tell him he doesn't have to do everything Alta says? Michelle thought.

No, she thought. He volunteered. He's not doing anything he doesn't want to do.

Catherine wandered by. "Hi, guys. I just wanted to tell you all that we have a really fun craft project this afternoon. We've got all the stuff you need to make your own comic books. Come check it out."

"Let's do it. That sounds fun," Mandy said.

"Yeah. Come on, everyone," Alta answered. She started toward the craft table.

"Oh, Marshall," she called over her shoulder. "Would you throw away all that trash?" She pointed to the empty soda cans, orange peels, crushed potato chips, and brown paper bags covering their lunch table.

"Sure," Marshall replied.

"I'll help," Michelle said quickly. She gathered the soda cans and threw them in the recycling bin.

Cassie and Mandy grabbed some trash and threw it away. Alta shook her head at them. "That's what Marshall's for," she said. Then she headed for the craft table.

Michelle and the others followed her. Marshall sat down next to Michelle. Then he stood back up. He dragged his chair a few feet away from her and sat down again.

What is he doing? Michelle thought.

Oh, yeah, she realized. Rule number seven. That's *Don't hang all over me. Stay at least three feet away.*

Michelle glanced over at her cousin. He was already working hard on his comic book. He looked totally caught up in it.

What should I do my comic book about? Michelle thought. Maybe something about Christmas, she thought. Something with Santa in it. Santa the Superhero!

Michelle grabbed a red pen and started to draw. She gave Santa a big *S* on the front of his outfit.

"This is hard," Cassie said. "I can't think of anything."

"Why not do something about your dog?" Michelle asked. "Okay is so cute." Okay was Cassie's dachshund.

"That's a good idea," Cassie answered. "He already looks like something out of a comic book. His body is so long, and his legs are so short!"

Michelle giggled. "You're right," she said. She started working on her Santa comic book again.

Maybe I'll give this to my dad for Christmas, Michelle thought. He loves my drawings. She put the red pen back in the center of the table and grabbed the green one. I'd better work fast so I'll finish in time.

"I'm done," Marshall announced about an hour later.

"Can I see?" Michelle asked.

"Well . . ." Marshall hesitated. Then he smiled. He handed Michelle his book.

Michelle read the front cover. *"Attack of the Killer Cockroaches."* Figures, she thought.

She flipped it open. The drawings were good. Really good.

"I didn't know you could draw like this, Marshall," she exclaimed. "This is great."

Marshall shrugged. "Cartooning is my favorite thing—after bugs," he explained.

Michelle began to read. The comic book was all about a kid on a space mission who got separated from his family and wound up on a planet inhabited by alien bugs. The bugs tortured the kid.

The kid looked exactly like Marshall. The leader of the bugs looked familiar too. It had glittering red and green claws. And curly black hair.

It looks like Alta! Michelle realized.

She kept reading. A superhero ladybug helped the kid fight off the evil alien bugs.

Hey, that ladybug is me, Michelle thought.

Except in real life I didn't help Marshall when Alta was mean to him, she thought. I told myself that he didn't mind her bossing him around. And I'm the one who told Marshall to be nice to her.

Michelle stared down at the drawing of Alta the alien bug torturing Marshall the Earth kid. She started feeling sort of sick.

"Marshall, I—" Michelle said.

Alta interrupted. "Marshall, I wanted to say thanks for all the stuff you've done for me today."

Marshall gave a tiny smile. "You do?" he asked.

Good, Michelle thought. Alta *should* thank Marshall.

"Uh-huh. And I want you to come to my party," Alta said.

Oh, wow! This is so great! Michelle grinned at Cassie and Mandy.

"Is Michelle invited again?" Marshall asked.

"Of course!" Alta said. "You'll come, won't you, Michelle?"

"Definitely!" Michelle cried.

Alta picked up a green pen and went back to work on her comic book. "This is out of ink! Marshall, would you get me another one?"

Michelle heard Marshall give a tiny sigh. He stood up.

No way! Michelle thought. I can't let Alta keep bossing Marshall around.

"There's another green pen at the end of the table," Michelle said. "Can't you just get it yourself?"

"I want Marshall to do it," Alta told her. "If he doesn't get me the pen, then he can't come to my party!"

Chapter

14

♥ "Marshall isn't getting you the pen!" Michelle declared.

"Then he's not going to the party," Alta snapped.

Michelle stood up and put her hands on her hips. "Fine. He's not going. And neither am I!"

"Me either!" Cassie added.

"Or me!" Mandy called.

Alta's mouth opened. Then closed. Then opened again. "You are all going to miss the most awesome party ever!" she cried. She got up and stomped away.

Michelle smiled at Marshall. "Yay! We beat the horrible alien bug," she exclaimed. Marshall gave her a high-five.

"One, two, three—go!"

Marshall swung the baseball bat at the Santa piñata. He missed.

"Keep trying!" Michelle yelled.

"You can do it!" Cassie called.

"Wait, let me fix your blindfold," Danny said. He hurried up and tightened the handkerchief around Marshall's eyes.

"This is the best Christmas party ever!" Mandy said. "I bet we're having way more fun than everyone who is at Alta's party right now."

"Yeah," Cassie agreed. "I love these weird bug cookies Marshall made. They are great with eggnog." She took a sip.

"Swing, Marshall!" Michelle yelled.

Marshall took another swing at the piñata—and missed.

"Try again!" Mandy cried.

"Break open the piñata! So we can have some candy!" Cassie shouted.

Nicky and Alex jumped up and down, still dressed in the reindeer outfits they wore for their play. "Hit it! Hit it!" they shouted.

Whoosh! The bat swept through the air. Marshall missed.

Whoosh! He missed again.

CRASH!

Cassie and Mandy squealed.

"Oh, no!" Michelle cried. "Marshall, you just broke your ant farm!"

"Ants, ants, ants!" the twins screamed.

"All over my house," Danny moaned. "I'll get a jar we can put them in." He dashed out of the living room.

Marshall ripped off his blindfold. "Don't step on Michelle!" he yelled. "She's my favorite ant!"

"No, I'm your favorite *cousin*," Michelle said.

"Yeah, you are my favorite cousin." Marshall grinned at her.

Danny ran back into the room with a big jar in his hands. He stared at the ground so he wouldn't step on any of the ants.

Bam! He smashed into the piñata. It burst open—and candy flew everywhere!

A chocolate kiss sailed past Michelle. She caught it, peeled off the silver wrapping, and popped the candy into her mouth.

"Aaagh! The ants are climbing up my leg!" Mandy yelled.

"I'll get them!" Marshall lunged forward—and knocked into Cassie.

Splash! Cassie's eggnog landed on the floor.

Here we go again! Michelle thought. She started to laugh, as she helped scoop up the ants. Oh, well, at least with Marshall around, my Christmas vacation wasn't ho-ho-ho-hum!

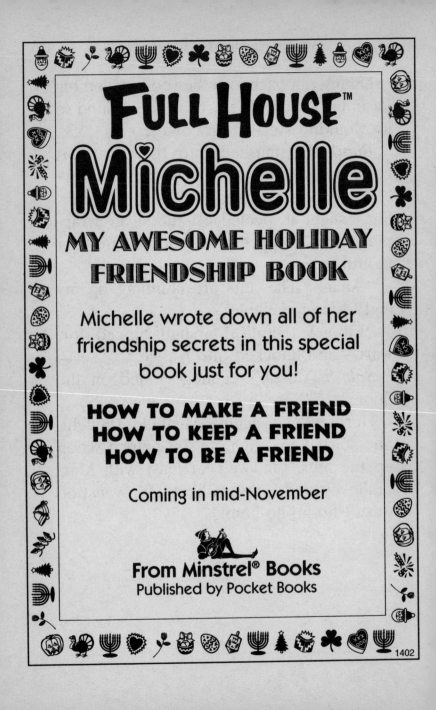

FULL HOUSE™

Michelle

MY AWESOME HOLIDAY FRIENDSHIP BOOK

Michelle wrote down all of her friendship secrets in this special book just for you!

HOW TO MAKE A FRIEND
HOW TO KEEP A FRIEND
HOW TO BE A FRIEND

Coming in mid-November

From Minstrel® Books
Published by Pocket Books

1402

It doesn't matter if you live around the corner...
or around the world...
If you are a fan of Mary-Kate and Ashley Olsen,
you should be a member of

MARY-KATE + ASHLEY'S FUN CLUB™

Here's what you get:
Our Funzine™
An autographed color photo
Two black & white individual photos
A full size color poster
An official **Fun Club**™ membership card
A **Fun Club**™ school folder
Two special **Fun Club**™ surprises
A holiday card
Fun Club™ collectibles catalog
Plus a **Fun Club**™ box to keep everything in

To join Mary-Kate + Ashley's Fun Club™, fill out the form
below and send it along with

U.S. Residents – $17.00
Canadian Residents – $22 U.S. Funds
International Residents – $27 U.S. Funds

**MARY-KATE + ASHLEY'S FUN CLUB™
859 HOLLYWOOD WAY, SUITE 275
BURBANK, CA 91505**

NAME:_____

ADDRESS:_____

_CITY:_____ STATE:_____ ZIP:_____

PHONE:(____) _____ BIRTHDATE:_____

1242

FULL HOUSE™
Stephanie

PHONE CALL FROM A FLAMINGO	88004-7/$3.99
THE BOY-OH-BOY NEXT DOOR	88121-3/$3.99
TWIN TROUBLES	88290-2/$3.99
HIP HOP TILL YOU DROP	88291-0/$3.99
HERE COMES THE BRAND NEW ME	89858-2/$3.99
THE SECRET'S OUT	89859-0/$3.99
DADDY'S NOT-SO-LITTLE GIRL	89860-4/$3.99
P.S. FRIENDS FOREVER	89861-2/$3.99
GETTING EVEN WITH THE FLAMINGOES	52273-6/$3.99
THE DUDE OF MY DREAMS	52274-4/$3.99
BACK-TO-SCHOOL COOL	52275-2/$3.99
PICTURE ME FAMOUS	52276-0/$3.99
TWO-FOR-ONE CHRISTMAS FUN	53546-3/$3.99
THE BIG FIX-UP MIX-UP	53547-1/$3.99
TEN WAYS TO WRECK A DATE	53548-X/$3.99
WISH UPON A VCR	53549-8/$3.99
DOUBLES OR NOTHING	56841-8/$3.99
SUGAR AND SPICE ADVICE	56842-6/$3.99
NEVER TRUST A FLAMINGO	56843-4/$3.99
THE TRUTH ABOUT BOYS	00361-5/$3.99
CRAZY ABOUT THE FUTURE	00362-3/$3.99
MY SECRET ADMIRER	00363-1/$3.99
BLUE RIBBON CHRISTMAS	00830-7/$3.99

Available from Minstrel® Books Published by Pocket Books